Marky

Missy

Mrs. Stevens

Mr. Stevens

Marky
& The Cat

Sally Anne

John David

First Edition.   10 9 8 7 6 5 4 3 2 1

Text © 1998, Illustrations © 1999 Blessing Our World, Inc.

First Printing 2000

Illustrations are water color style

Book design by Janet Long.

Body copy typeface is KidPrint Bold.
Title typefaces are Quaint and Tenace Regular

Publishers Cataloging-in-Publication Data
Prepared by Blessing Our World, Inc.

Library of Congress Card Number: 99-091778

Luke, Deanna, 1948–

Marky and The Cat / by Deanna Luke; illustrated by Lynne Chambers

Marky and The Cat is a series story of a boy and his adventures with his family and friends. His cat teaches Marky about surprises. For children, ages 7–11.

LCCN 99-091778 ISBN 1-928777-06-6

[1. Picture Books for Children 2. Prose and Children]
I. Chambers, Lynne, Ill.   II. Title

Printed in Hong Kong

Published 2000 by
SAN 299-8920
Blessing Our World, Inc.
P.O. Box 642
Palestine, Texas 75802-0642

Protecting the Minds
of Our Future

Visit our website at http://www.blessworld.com

Written by
Deanna Luke

Illustrated by
Lynne Chambers

Designed by
Janet Long

Blessing Our World, Inc.

P.O. Box 642 • Palestine, Texas 75802-0642

Hi! My name is Marky. Marky Stevens, that is. My sister can be so silly. Her friends are, too. They come in the den where I'm watching TV to whisper, then giggle and run.

Willie my cat is a great big, gray tomcat.

You can hear
every word they
say when they
whisper. I can't
figure out if
they are sillier
than they used to
be, or not. Mom says
that's just how girls are.
But Mom's not like that.

Willie likes to go out and
wander around like all
tomcats.

Mom....

SALLY ANNE...

I am sure Dad is glad that Mom isn't like that. He likes it when Mom takes care of stuff and she sure couldn't do that if she acted all silly like Missy and her friends. I bet Mom was a lot like Sally Anne when she was a girl.

Sometimes I worry when Willie goes out at night, but Mom and Dad say that is what all tomcats do.

Missy still likes some dude named
John David. He's older than she
is by a lot. He's nearly fourteen
and she's only been eleven for
seven months. Mom will trip when
she finds out.

Willie has come back
bunged up a few times
after being out all night.

If John David really knew how silly my sister can act, he wouldn't like her anyway. Someone can just say his name and she flops down on the furniture like she might faint.

One time Willie was gone for two and a half days, so we thought he was dead.

It seems like to me that Missy would be very embarrassed about acting like that all the time. My dad told me I might like a silly girl like Missy someday. I told my dad, "No way!"

I went out with Dad looking everywhere for Willie, but we couldn't find him. Dad said Willie would find his own way home when he was ready.

I wish Missy would... faint, that is. It would be a lot quieter around here. She goes on about stuff no one cares about. She giggles all the time. She likes to boss me around to beat the band.

Willie was sort of scratched up when he finally got home.

One day I was just minding my own business, and she made me come in the house to pick up my socks. Mom never has to tell me what to do 'cause Missy always beats her to it. Missy just likes to send me on wild goose chases.

Willie looked worse than ever this time after he'd been fighting.

Like one day, Missy
sent me to my room to
make up my bed. When
I got there, it was
already made. I can't
believe I fell for that.

I knew she was in the
kitchen laughing at me. Boy,
she makes me real mad.

I bet Willie won the fight even if
he got all messed up doing it,
'cause he's a tough tomcat.

Mom feels sorry for me, I can tell, when Missy does that stuff. Dad keeps telling me to learn how to ignore her, but it is too hard. I wish I could grow up and *be* older than she is someday.

I never have actually seen Willie when he is having a fight, but you can tell he would never be afraid of another cat.

Missy invited John David over to our house. That's fine for her, and he can meet Mom and Dad. But what am I supposed to do with myself? Disappear?

Mom had to really bandage up poor Ol' Willie this time.

She'd like that. Just look up
and I'm gone. Disappeared
forever. Then she could
have everything her
way. Well, no such
luck. I'm going to
watch John David.
Dad will croak if he
puts his arm around
Missy. John David is
old so I know he will.

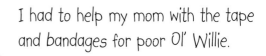

I had to help my mom with the tape
and bandages for poor Ol' Willie.

I wonder if John David likes sports. I bet he would rather be playing baseball with me than sitting around talking to Missy and Mom and Dad. I don't think I ever want to go to some girl's house and try to figure out what to say to her and her parents.

Willie has to stay in for a few weeks until he heals up some, 'cause he can't defend himself all bandaged up.

When I came in from *baseball* practice, John David was already there. That's why Jeffy gave me a ride. Missy planned this *so* I'd be gone when he came. Well, I fooled her, 'cause here I am. And it's even *better*, because I smell like a wet dog. She'll fuss about that! I'm glad.

Ol' Willie is gettin fat lying around the house.

John David and Dad were watching a baseball game in the den. Mom and Missy were in the kitchen clattering around. They were fixing snacks. "How was practice, Slugger?" Dad asked me. I shrugged and said, "OK, I guess," and sat down to watch the game.

Willie sleeps like half the time now, I hope he's not sick.

John David isn't so bad. He's a lot better than Missy. I guess it would be too much to ask to just have him and let her go live with someone else. She doesn't giggle when he's around. Maybe he told her not to act so silly. If he did, I really owe him one!

Mom took Willie to the vet today to see why he's so tired all the time.

John David asked Missy to go out on the patio with him when the game was over. They talked for a few minutes, and then Missy came running in the house all smiles and asked me where Mom was.

Mom didn't tell me what the vet said when she brought Willie back in the house, but she was sure being careful with him.

I heard Missy telling Mom that John David had invited her to go to the eighth grade dance. She's gonna look so dumb with all those older kids. I cannot believe Mom and Dad are going to let her go. Sometimes I wonder what the big deal is about dating anyway.

Willie got his bandages off, but he still can't go outside.

When I get to the eighth grade, I sure won't like some silly sixth grader for a girlfriend. I probably won't like girls at all except Sally Anne. She's my friend. She likes the same stuff I do.

Mom made Ol' mean Willie a real soft bed.

Missy and Mom are going shopping for a dress and shoes for the dance. I hope they don't make me go. Shopping isn't my favorite thing to do. Maybe Dad and I will go fishing or something instead.

Mom picked up poor Ol' Willie and put him in the new soft bed so he would know it was for him.

Sally Anne likes
my tree house
and lemonade
stands. She
even likes
playing with my
electric train.
When Ol' Jack
Martin and I chunk
pinecones at girls and
cats, I always miss
Sally Anne with my
pinecone on purpose.
Then I say, "Shucks."

Willie went right to
sleep.

Dad told me I would need to let Willie just rest in his bed for a while.

Mom and Missy came in all excited about her new blue dress that was just the perfect dress for the eighth grade dance. That dress must have cost a lot of money.

Willie has come into my room the last two nights to sleep on the foot of my bed.

I hate to admit it,
but Missy looked
okay.

John David came to pick up Missy for the dance. His dad drove them. It wasn't like a real date, because John David isn't old enough to drive a car yet.

I had to be really careful when Willie was sleeping on the bed with me.

He did bring her a flower and she gave him one. He wore it! Yech! I'll never get used to some things. It seems like flowers are okay for girls. But not for guys! When John David came in the door and Missy held his hand, Dad's face turned a little red.

And when John David put his arm around Missy's waist, I thought Dad was going to faint. I just had to smile a little.

Willie woke me up in the night and I thought he was acting sort of funny.

Mom explained to me after they left that someday I would wear flowers and be happy about it. I'm not sure about that.

I went to wake my mom up to check on Willie. When we went back in my room, HE had four little kittens. I think I'll give Sally Anne one.

My dad said even he had worn flowers lots of times. I asked him why. He told me it was a nice thing to do for formal occasions like dances and weddings.

WILLIE...

WILLEMENA

Mom said we'd have to change Willie's name to Willemena.

Dad pulled out his wallet and showed me a picture of him all dressed up and my mom in a white dress. She had a bunch of flowers in her hands, and Dad had a flower pinned on his coat just like the flower Missy had gotten John David for the dance.

I'd say life is full of surprises, Willemena
and her kittens are proof of that!

The End

About the Author

Deanna Luke has been writing since her youth. She is married to Jerry, and they have three daughters, Sunny, Keily, and Jennifer, and a son-in-law, Steve. They have four grandchildren, Nicole, Miles, Susannah, and Timothy. When her grandchildren were born Deanna began to look at several of her books for publishing. It is her desire for all children to have an opportunity to read books that offer excitement and pleasure as well as good morals and values. She graduated from Emmaus Road Ministry School in 1992. She has studied creative writing at the University of Texas in Tyler as well as private writers' conferences across the United States. She is dedicated to the Lord and the generational transfer of His love through her writing. She currently resides in Texas.

About the Illustrator

Lynne Chambers received her Bachelor of Arts Degree in Advertising with a minor in Art from San Jose State University in San Jose, California. Lynne has always included her art in various aspects of her life, creating free-form art, graphics and design, mural design, greeting cards and book illustration. Lynne desires at this time in her life to create for the Lord, applying her talent toward the generational transfer of the love of the Lord Jesus Christ.

About the Designer

Janet Long has a degree in advertising art and she spent the first ten years of her career in advertising. Her great love of books has led her to spend the last thirteen years as a freelance designer and illustrator of children's, educational and craft books.